llllll
llllll
llllll
love

To:

From:

lots of love

little one

forever and always

sourcebooks jabberwocky

by Sandra Magsamen

You're a gift and a blessing in every way. I love you more each and every day!

I love you more than all the stars that twinkle at night,

and all the fireflies that glow

so bright.

I love **you**
more than
all the
spaghetti
served in
Rome,

and more than each and every dog loves her bone.

I love you more than all the languages spoken in the world,

and more

dan

that

than all the **cers**
have ever
twirled.

I love **YOU** more than all the sweet **kisses** that have ever been given,

and more than all the miles every car has been driven.

I love you more than all the adventures you have ahead,

and more
than all the
peanut butter
and jelly
spread
on bread!

I love YOU so much, my Precious little one.

You are a **light** in my life, like the moon and the sun.

I'll love you as you sleep at night and play through the days.

I'll love
you yesterday,
today, forever
and
always.

**Big heartfelt thanks to Karen Botti and Hannah Magsamen Barry.
Their creativity and generous spirits are unique and valued gifts
to me and the work we create in the studio.**

Published by Sourcebooks Jabberwocky, an imprint of Sourcebooks, Inc.
P.O. Box 4410, Naperville, Illinois 60567-4410
(630) 961-3900
Fax: (630) 961-2168
sourcebooks.com

Library of Congress Cataloging-in-Publication Data is on file with the publisher.

Source of Production: 1010 Printing International, Kowloon, Hong Kong, China
Date of Production: September 2018
Run Number: 5013077

Printed and bound in China.
OGP 10 9 8 7 6 5 4 3 2 1